Y0-AGA-195

STORIES ABOUT THE
BLACK
EXPERIENCE

ROBERT L. BRADLEY

VOLUME

THE LORD WILL MAKE A WAY

ONE

The stories in this book are fictional. The characters in these stories are fictitious and exist nowhere but in the author's imagination, and if they happen to have the same names as actual persons, it is a coincidence. When an actual person's name such as an author or a singer is mentioned in a story, it is mentioned only to make the story more realistic. The places in these stories are both real and imaginary. Real places are used in a fictional way. Names of things in these stories are used in a fictional way. Dates have been added to these stories to give a meaning to them.

FIRST EDITION

First printing, 2001

Published by
Robert L. Bradley
P.O. Box 25768
St. Louis, Missouri 63136

ISBN 0-9702912-0-5

Library of Congress Control Number (LCCN): 00-091905

Cover illustration by Sharon Morton

*This book is dedicated to my wife, Rosilyn;
son, Michael; and daughters, Alicia and Janae.*

ACKNOWLEDGEMENTS

This book would not have become a reality without the support and kindness of others.

Special thanks to my wife Rosilyn for reading the stories in this book and giving me her frank opinion.

Deep appreciation to Gwendolyn Whiteside for taking the time to edit this book. Her kindness and generosity are appreciated so very much.

Special thanks to sisters Betty Bradley, Sennie Bradley, Bobbie Bonner, and Roxie Turner for their interest in this book.

Special thanks also to nieces Melba Bradley and Trina Bradley for their interest in this book.

Special appreciation to artist Sharon Morton for the cover illustration of this book.

CONTENTS

INTRODUCTION

Since time immemorial blacks have been a very spiritual and religious people. They created the ancient Nile Valley religions, which were practiced by Africans for thousands of years. When the religions of Christianity and Islam arose, Africans also played a role in their development and spread.

The sixteenth century marked the beginning of black enslavement in the Americas, which lasted nearly 400 years. This enslavement period was filled with pain and suffering for black people. One way slaves were able to cope with the pain and suffering of slavery was through songs such as "There's a Great Camp Meeting in the Promised Land," "Sabbath Has No End," and "Steal Away to Jesus," which enabled the slaves to escape their pain and suffering spiritually. Through the singing of these religious songs, the slaves were able to transcend their earthly plane of oppression on the plantation to a spiritual plane of peace and happiness, where every day was Sabbath and one could walk around heaven all day and do nothing but sing and shout.

The slaves also relied on prayer as a source of strength and inspiration. It would lift their spirits when they became tired and weary from the rigorous plantation life. It would give them the strength to go on after watching their family members being sold away from them. However, according to stories that have been passed down from slavery, some slavemasters didn't want to see their slaves praying, and if they caught them praying, they would whip them. To avoid being whipped, some slaves would sneak and pray under a big, black washpot, which kept their voices from being heard. Others would steal away to their little, secret praying grounds in the woods or cane fields to pray. At their secret praying grounds, whether under a washpot or in the woods, the slaves would call on the Lord and tell Him all about their troubles.

The black experience, as defined here, is a story of black people's struggle to overcome hard times and adversity in America from slavery times to the present. Faced with overwhelming odds, black people have stumbled at times along the way, but they have never given up. The black experience is African-Americans surviving the most dehumanizing and brutal slavery known to man. The black experience is a poorly educated African-American woman who raises nine children in a crime-infested housing project and they all turn out to be successful adults. The black experience is an African-American boy who overcomes juvenile delinquency and a speech problem to become a successful man. The black experience is an African-American man who works three jobs to support his large family. The black experience is Wilma Rudolph overcoming polio as a kid to become an internationally known track star, winning three gold medals in the 1960 Olympic games. The black experience is Harriet Tubman risking her life numerous times in leading over 300 slaves to freedom in the North. The black experience is legendary boxer Muhammad Ali bouncing back again and again from setbacks and failures during his illustrious boxing career. The black experience is Martin Luther King, Jr. and other civil rights workers' bitter struggle to desegregate Birmingham, Alabama in 1963, where they faced snarling dogs, high-powered water hoses, and prejudiced policemen, but they refused to give up and won in the end. The black experience is Jackie Robinson's resiliency, perseverance, and courage in the face of unrelenting hostilities in 1948 when he desegregated major league baseball. In short, the black experience is these examples and many, many more.

There are many African-Americans who have responded positively to hard times and adversity. When hard times and adversity occurred, they faced it and overcame it, instead of giving up. In fact, some of them seem to thrive on hard times and adversity. There is perhaps nothing more gratifying than facing and overcoming hard times and adversity.

I have lived the black experience. I grew up in a broken home and was raised on hard times. Getting an education was a struggle for me from elementary school to graduate school. Life has presented me with many challenges, and I have tried to deal with them the best way that I could. Having a strong, caring, and wise mother helped me in many ways. Without her support, I probably would not have made it.

In elementary school I heard some inspirational words from a track coach named Clarence Higgins, who I have never forgotten. He was pushing us hard and some of the track team members began to complain. In response, he gave us some words of wisdom and inspiration that have been with me ever since. He said to us, " A quitter never wins and a winner never quits." I had never heard that expression before, but it made a lot of sense to me. I was in the fifth grade then and called myself running track. Henceforth, I have tried to finish everything that I have started.

In the sixth grade I had a teacher named Miss Obie Bell Harding and she always stressed the value of a good education. It seems like she encouraged us almost every day to come to school so we could get a good education. She didn't like for us to be absent from school. She told us that machines were phasing out manual labor and when we were grown we would need a good education to get a good job. That made a lot of sense to me. I made up my mind then that I was going to get myself a good education no matter how hard I had to struggle to get it.

Living the black experience has prepared me to write about the black experience. This book consists of five fictional stories about the black experience. These stories deal with people who overcome hard times and adversity through the power of hope and faith. People born with a silver spoon in their mouths or who have had an easy life may not be able to identify with these "spiritual stories," but on the other hand, if you have had to deal with hard times and adversity, you will most certainly be able to identify with them.

I hope these stories have a positive influence on the reader. If the reader is experiencing an adverse condition such as loneliness, hopelessness, poverty, imprisonment, sickness, or drug addiction, I hope these stories give him or her the strength and inspiration to overcome.

If you believe it,
you can see it

▼▼

CHARLIE WILLIAMS, A SOPHOMORE IN HIGH SCHOOL, WAS SO EXCITED as he went to his last period English class. He thought to himself, "I'm going to ask Mary Jenkins if she will go to the Mid-South Fair with me next week. I've liked this cute, little girl with the dimples in her cheeks since I first saw her last year in the ninth grade. The way she looks at me, I believe she likes me too."

Mary Jenkins did like Charlie. She had been admiring the tall, muscular Charlie since last year.

After the English class was over, Charlie asked Mary if she would go to the fair with him. She answered with a big smile, "Charlie, I will be glad to go to the fair with you."

It was the fall of 1951 when Charlie Williams and Mary Jenkins went to the Mid-South Fair in Memphis, Tennessee. They had so much fun together at the fair, walking and talking, laughing, eating, and riding various amusement rides. Charlie and Mary continued to date the rest of the fall, going to school dances and football games. During the winter they enjoyed going to basketball games together in the school gym. When spring rolled around, they could be seen laughing and talking as they walked hand-in-hand from school every day. By summer Charlie and Mary had fallen deeply in love with each other and were inseparable. When they returned to high school for their junior year, the fall of 1952, their courtship had blossomed to the point that they were talking marriage, and they both were only sixteen.

Charlie and Mary were hesitant at first about telling their parents that they wanted to drop out of high school to get married. But on Thanksgiving Day they finally told them. Charlie's mother and father were surprised at the news and pleaded with them to wait until they finished high school and had jobs before they got married. Mary's Aunt Alice, who had raised her since her mother died, was equally surprised at the news and also pleaded with them to wait until they finished high school and had jobs before they got married. But Charlie and Mary were so much in love that they couldn't wait and they got married on Christmas Day, 1952.

Charlie was from a large family; he had eight brothers and five sisters. Mary had two brothers and a sister. Her mother had died when she was three years old and she had never known her father. Since her mother's death, Mary had been raised by her mother's sister, Aunt Alice, who had seven children of her own. Having been raised in a large family, both Charlie and Mary also wanted a large family.

Charlie was only sixteen years old, but he was as big and tall as a grown man. He, therefore, didn't have any problem getting hired as a laborer at a factory. It was decided by mutual consent that Mary wouldn't work. She would remain at home and be a housewife.

In January of 1953 the excited couple moved into an apartment in North Memphis and began their life together as husband and wife. In January of 1954 their first child, James, was born. Time moved fast and by 1960 Charlie and Mary had six children, including a set of twin girls. When a seventh child was born a year later, Charlie decided it was time to leave the apartment and buy him a home. To help pay his house note, he got a second job working in a grocery store on weekends.

The Williams family continued to grow. In 1965 a set of twin boys was born to Charlie and Mary, giving them twelve children, six boys and six girls. They both, however, liked children and saw their large family as a blessing from God rather than as a liability. To help provide for his large family, Charlie found a third job cleaning up an office building after he got off of his main job at the factory at 3:00 p.m.

In addition to being a large family, the Williams family was also a close-knit and happy family. They enjoyed doing things together. They especially looked forward to going to church together every Sunday. And after church they always came home to that big, down-home delicious Southern dinner.

Meanwhile, Charlie continued to work his three jobs. He felt he needed to do it in order to bring in extra money to support his large family. One day, however, Mary noticed that he looked tired and said, "Charlie, I believe you are working too hard. You need to stop working that third job so you can rest in the evening after getting off your main job."

Charlie answered, "Mary, I am a little tired but I can make it. I'm going to work this third job one more year and then I'm going to quit it. We need the extra money."

Mary said, "Charlie, we can make it without the third job. You need to quit now. You look tired."

Charlie replied, "Mary, don't worry about me. I'll be all right."

Unable to get Charlie to quit working the third job, Mary sort of gave up for the time being. But she still was worried about Charlie. He looked tired and seemed to be pushing himself too hard.

One morning about three months later, Mary was washing dishes in the kitchen when she heard the telephone ring. She picked up the telephone and a man told her that Charlie had had a massive heart attack at work and had died on the way to the hospital. The tragic news stunned Mary, she couldn't believe that Charlie was gone.

The sudden death of Charlie brought grief and pain to Mary, his children, relatives, and friends. After the funeral family members and friends gathered at Mary's house to help console her and her children, and to offer them their support. Charlie had been a good husband, a caring father, and had always been there when his family needed him. He would be truly missed.

The responsibility of providing for twelve children had now fallen on Mary's shoulders. She was aware that providing for twelve children would be a struggle but she believed she could do it. She was also aware that she would have to remain strong no matter what happened if she and her kids were going to make it. Mary was too proud to go on welfare. She, therefore, got a job as a maid working in a hotel. Her sister Betty kept her children that were too young to attend school. The first year was relatively easy for Mary and her children because of the support they got from relatives and friends, who gave them food, clothing, and money. But at the beginning of the second year times got tough as support from relatives and friends dwindled considerably. With mainly her maid job to support the family, Mary was unable to pay the mortgage and lost her home. This forced the Williams family to move to an apartment.

This was the first time that Mary and her children had ever struggled like this. People began to ask her, how was she going to make it with all those kids? Mary told them that the Lord was going to make a way for her and her kids. She began to pray to the Lord night and day asking Him to make things easier for her and her kids. Although hard times continued to test Mary and her kids, she never lost faith. She even looked for a better paying job but was unable to find one. Despite the adversity she faced, Mary kept on believing that God would answer her prayers.

One hot summer day in July of 1967, Mary felt so tired and weary as she rode a Memphis Transit Authority bus home from work. As usual, when she got home she opened her mailbox and got the mail out. To her surprise, there was a letter from Teresa Owens, an old friend from her high school days. Mary hurriedly opened the letter and read it. Her face broke into a smile when she finished reading it. Teresa, her old friend, was a successful lawyer down in New Orleans, Louisiana. She was also married and had two children. Teresa had heard about the death of Charlie and how rough a time Mary was having supporting her kids, and she wanted to help her. She wanted Mary and her kids to come to New Orleans where she was and she would help her get a good job. Mary answered Teresa's letter and in the letter she told her that she and the kids were coming to New Orleans immediately. Mary was very excited; her prayers had finally been answered.

In August, Mary and her twelve children were moved to New Orleans by her older brother Issac. When they arrived at Teresa and her family's beautiful home, they were greeted very warmly by them. True to her word, Teresa helped Mary to get a good paying job. It was working as a domestic cook for a very wealthy white family, which paid very well. In early October Mary and her children moved out of Teresa's home into a home of their own. Mary and her children liked New Orleans and adapted to it rather quickly. They found a friendly, little church to attend and in school the children did very well. By the summer of the next year, 1968, Mary had saved enough money to make a down payment on a used 1966 Chevrolet station wagon. Mary and her children now lived comfortably. The best they had lived since Charlie's death. They were buying a car and a home; they were wearing decent clothes; they had plenty of food to eat; and they had some extra money to spend. Mary also was trying to save some money but it was hard to do with such a large family.

Things continued to go well for Mary and her family as the year 1969 rolled in. Mary was so happy that she and the kids were doing well that a day didn't go by without her thanking God for her blessings.

In June of 1969 Mary's sister Betty came to New Orleans to visit her and the kids. This was the first time that they had seen any of their relatives in almost two years. They were very happy to see Betty. Her visit lasted two weeks and when she left, Mary suddenly realized how much she missed her relatives back in Memphis. For a week, Mary wrestled with the thought of remaining in New Orleans or returning to Memphis. In the end, homesickness won out and she told her kids that they were moving back to Memphis.

Mary also told her employer, her friend Teresa, and friends and neighbors that she and the kids were moving back to Memphis. They tried to talk her into changing her mind, but her mind was firmly made up and they couldn't talk her into remaining in New Orleans.

In early July Mary and her twelve children arrived in Memphis. They brought along with them the car, food and clothing, furniture, and other items, but very little money. Mary was hoping that her relatives could help her financially. Unfortunately, however, she returned home at a bad time. Most of her relatives were struggling themselves and were barely making it. Times were hard, and they just didn't have the money to help her get started again.

Some relatives even said that Mary and her kids should have

stayed down in New Orleans, where they had done well.

When Mary asked some of her relatives could she and the kids stay with them temporarily, they told her that they would like to help her, but she had so many kids that they didn't have the extra room to accommodate them. To solve the problem, Cousin Bennie suggested that Mary split up her twelve children into small groups, let two kids stay with one relative, let three kids stay with another relative, and so on. Mary told him that she loved her children too much to split them up and she was going to keep them all together. She also told him if she and her kids couldn't find anywhere to stay, they would rather walk the streets together than to be divided from each other.

"We know that a good mother loves her children all the time and will stick by them through thick and thin."

Meanwhile, when Mary's Aunt Alice, who had raised her, learned that Mary and her children didn't have anywhere to stay, she was moved to tears. She told Mary that her house was crowded but she would make room for them; she wasn't going to let them walk the streets.

Within a month, Mary found a job working as a domestic maid. She and her kids then moved into a housing project where the rent was cheap. But she refused to go on welfare, saying that as long as she had her health and strength, she would rather work than to be supported by the state.

Although Mary was working, she barely made enough money for her kids to have food and clothing. Every day was a struggle to survive. She often went to the goodwill to buy her children used clothes to wear. She couldn't afford to throw away leftover food. She would turn leftover rice into a delicious rice pudding or leftover bread into a tasty bread pudding. When her children's shoes got holes in the bottoms, she couldn't afford to throw them away; instead she would put cardboard in the bottoms of the shoes so they could continue to wear them.

Mary was a very spiritual woman and when she was low in spirits she would often sing to lift her spirits. Sometimes she would be in the kitchen washing dishes, rattling the pots and pans, and she would begin singing the song "The Lord Will Make a Way Somehow." This was her favorite song; she drew strength and inspiration from it. It gave her the strength to go on when she felt tired and weary. It gave her the inspiration to continue to believe she could make it when she felt like giving up. She also believed deeply in this song. She believed that the Lord was going to make a way somehow for her and her children.

Nevertheless, hard times continued for Mary and her children. The winter of 1970-71 was especially rough. Mary got behind on her bills and ended up having her car and some of her furniture repossessed. This troubled Mary and she would sometimes lay in bed at night tossing and turning, worrying about how she was going to pay her bills, and unable to sleep. To ease her burden, she would get up out of her bed and fall down on her knees and talk to the Lord, telling Him all about her troubles. She felt that she could never pray too late to the Lord nor too often because He would always be there to listen to her prayers.

Mary and her children made it through the rough winter of 1970-71 thanks to their strong faith in God and to their determination.

Despite the hard times she was facing, Mary kept on believing that times would get better and they did. She began looking for a better paying job in the spring and by summer, she had found one. It was a job working as a cook at a big, prestigious restaurant. The restaurant's manager allowed her to take home all of the leftover food she wanted since she had twelve kids to feed. Mary impressed the manager with her hard work and cooking skills. And when the chief cook retired in December, the manager promoted her to his position, which paid very well. By March of 1972 she had saved enough money to make a down payment on a used 1970 Plymouth station wagon. In May her first-born child, James, graduated from high school and enlisted in the U.S. Army. The next year, 1973, her second-born child, Lester, graduated from high school and that fall he enrolled in college.

With things going so well, it seemed to Mary that time was flying by. In 1976 her twin girls, Alicia and Felicia, graduated from high school. In 1979 her son, Charlie Jr., graduated from high school. By 1983 all of her children had graduated from high school.

One summer day in 1985 Mary was busy cleaning her house when she began thinking about how blessed she was. She still had her job as chief cook at the restaurant where she had worked the last thirteen years. She had moved out of the housing project into a new home of her own. Her kids were all grown and doing well. James, the oldest, was out of the army, married, and working for the railroad. Lester had graduated from college and was married and teaching school. Patricia, her oldest daughter, was married and working for the government. Mitchell, another son, was in the navy. The twin girls, Alicia and Felicia, had graduated from college and were teaching school in Nashville, Tennessee. Her daughter Dorothy was married and working at a hospital. Her daughter Stephanie was married and living in Atlanta, Georgia. Linda, her youngest daughter, had graduated from college and was managing a supermarket. Her son, Charlie Jr., was a bricklayer and was working for a construction company. The twin boys, Larry and Barry, were working at a restaurant and living at home with her.

Things continued to go well for Mary the next two years but in 1987 trouble came knocking at her door. One Friday evening she was watching television when she heard the doorbell ring. She peeped through the window curtain to see who it was and it was her son James. She opened the door and he rushed in. He had a sad look on his face. Mary asked him what was wrong. He said, "Mama, I have just been fired from my job at the railroad, and I don't know what I am going to do. My supervisor said some things that upset me, and I lost my temper and hit him."

Mary replied, "Don't worry about it James; you can find yourself another job."

Mary's words seemed to uplift James and he said, "Mama, you are right. I'm going to start looking for myself another job next week."

James began looking for a job that Monday but after three months he still hadn't found a job. Frustrated, he stopped looking and began hanging out with some of his old buddies from high school. Unfortunately, these guys were into hustling and selling drugs. In a short while, James was also selling drugs, and making more money than he had ever made before. When James saw his twin brothers, Larry and Barry, he told them about the quick money he was making from selling drugs, and he asked them to come sell drugs with him so they could make them some quick money. His baby brothers were hesitant at first about joining him, but he kept telling them that they were working for peanuts at the restaurant and eventually they agreed to sell drugs with him. In addition to selling drugs, James and his twin brothers also got into selling hot items. And they made some good money from hustling. One day, however, they were on the corner selling some hot items from a store they had robbed, and were arrested by plainclothes policemen who had been secretly watching them.

When Mary heard that her three sons had been arrested, she was devastated. She couldn't believe that they had gotten into trouble with the law. She had raised them in the church and had always preached to them to avoid trouble and to do what was right.

James, Larry, and Barry were given ten years each for armed robbery and were sent to the state penitentiary. But due to some contacts Mary's boss had with some people in high places and her sons' good behavior, they were paroled after serving four years in prison.

Mary was so happy when James, Larry, and Barry came home from prison in 1993. She thought that prison life had taught them a lesson but she was sadly mistaken. They continued their "hustling lives and were in-and-out of jails all the time." A relative told Mary that her sons were grown men and no longer boys, and she should stop worrying about them. A neighbor told Mary to give up on her boys because they were incorrigible and no good. The same neighbor also told Mary that with her high blood pressure, worrying about her sons might bring on a fatal heart attack and she would be dead and gone, and her sons would still be alive "cutting the fool." Mary told her neighbor that she loved her sons too much to give up on them and she was going to stick by them to the end, and that she still believed God was going to turn their lives around.

"We know that a good mother loves her children all the time and will stick by them through thick and thin."

Meanwhile, James had really fallen apart now. In addition to living the life of a hustler, he was also strung out on drugs. This worried Mary and she prayed night and day for the Lord to turn his life around. She would say, "James, come go to church with me, son, so the Lord can turn your life around."

James would reply, "Mama, I'm coming to church." But he never came. He kept on living his self-destructive life.

When James wife, Sarah, learned that he was strung out on drugs, she was hurt and upset with him. She told him she still loved him, but that he had put her through so many changes, and had neglected her and his children so long that they couldn't live with him anymore. So they moved out of the house into an apartment.

One day James came by Mary's house and told her that he was going to Jackson, Mississippi on a business trip. It was raining and Mary told him to drive carefully. He said, "Mama, I will. I'm going to be careful."

But once he began driving toward Jackson, Mississippi he forgot what he had told her and started speeding. While speeding he hit a slick spot on the highway, lost control of his car, and turned over three times, but he miraculously escaped without a scratch. This incident shook James up. He knew that he could have been killed in the car accident. He believed that God was trying to talk to him.

The next Sunday James went back to the old church that he had joined as a kid. When he walked through the door, the church got so quiet that you could hear a pin fall and people began talking in hushed tones. James knew that they were talking about him but that was okay. He sat down and listened to the service and enjoyed it. The choir's songs were very uplifting. Deacon Hill's prayer was inspiring. Rev. Clark's sermon about the prodigal son touched James, transforming him into a state of spiritual ecstasy and he was moved to tears. And when Rev. Clark opened the doors of the church for people to join, James got up and gave a testimony. He told the congregation that he had experienced some rough times since he had last seen them. He told them that he had lost his job, he had been sent to prison for armed robbery, he had been in-and-out of jails for hustling, and his wife and children had walked off and left him because he had neglected them. He also told the congregation that he was strung out on drugs and had come back to rejoin the church so God could turn his life around. James was accepted back into the church and his mother was so happy that she was crying with tears of joy.

About six months after coming back to the church, James had

gotten himself together. A few months later he began preaching the gospel. His message was inspirational and very touching. James, knowing that he was responsible for leading his baby brothers down the path of self-destruction, went to them and had a soul-searching talk. His words inspired his twin brothers, Larry and Barry, to turn their lives around too. They quit the hustling life and enrolled in Henry's Technical School to study auto mechanics. After helping his twin brothers to turn their lives around, James went to his wife and children, and pleaded for forgiveness and one more chance as a father. They were moved by his emotional plea for forgiveness and forgave him, and gladly came back to live with him.

During the spring of 1997 James founded his own church and many people flocked to join it. He inspired all kinds of people with his spellbinding message of hope and faith. He told them if he could pull himself out of the "muck and mire" of self-destruction, they could too. James became sort of a hero to many youth back in the housing project where he had once lived.

Within a year after founding his own church, James opened a nice restaurant. It served good food and had a warm atmosphere. It became an over-night success, with James making lots of money.

On a warm, sunny day in early May of 2000 in Memphis, Mary Williams sat on her back porch with a look of happiness on her face. She was at peace now. Her sons James, Larry, and Barry had turned their lives around and were doing well. Her other children were also doing well. Sitting on the back porch with her were her two grandchildren, Janice and James Jr. They were her son James' kids. Earlier, Mary and her two grandchildren had been talking about the family reunion that was coming up in August, but now the subject had switched to raising children. Suddenly, James Jr. asked, "Grandmother, what kind of kid was Daddy?"

Mary replied, "Your father, James, was a good kid growing up; he got into trouble with the law when he got grown."

Janice then asked, "Grandmother, how did you manage to raise twelve children to adulthood without a husband and without going on welfare?"

Mary replied, "My children and I had some rough times. It wasn't easy having to provide for twelve children. But thanks to God's blessings, we made it. We made it on faith. Many times we didn't know where our next meal was going to come from, but we made it. If you believe in God, He will make a way for you. If you believe it, you can see it."

ANALYSIS OF STORY

This story "If You Believe It, You Can See It" illustrates the strength of the black family. Charlie was a hardworking and caring father, who gave the extra effort to support his large family. When he died his wife Mary inherited the job of being the family's breadwinner. With Mary as breadwinner, the family struggled at times, but it never gave up.

Mary was a strong, spiritual woman like many women in the black community, past and present. She successfully raised twelve children to adulthood after her husband's death, but not without experiencing hard times and adversity. Because of her strong faith in God, she refused to give up when faced with hard times and adversity and she won in the end.

There is power in believing. If you believe it, you can see it. Believing strongly that you can do something makes it easier to accomplish, because you won't give up when the going gets tough.

This story "If You Believe It, You Can See It" is dedicated to my mother in particular, who raised me and my sisters to adulthood after separating from my father, and to women in general who have raised children to adulthood without a husband.

A GOOD MOTHER

A good mother will stick by her
Children through thick and thin
No matter what her race
Or the color of her skin.

A good mother will love her
Children each and every day,
And she won't abandon them
If they go astray.

A son may cause his mother
Grief and pain,
But a good mother will
Love him just the same.

A daughter may run away
Or commit a crime,
But a good mother will
Still love her all the time.

A good mother will spank
Little Johnny if he's been bad at school
Because she doesn't want him
To grow up to be disobedient and rude.

A good mother will support
Her children all the time

Even if it means giving
Up her last dime.

Some ungrateful children take their good
Mother's love for granted and
Fail to help her when she gets old,
But these blind children don't realize
That their good mother's love is
Worth more than silver and gold.

Appreciate your good mother
Each and every day;
Don't wait until
She has passed away.

Robert L. Bradley, July 14, 1997

The Story of Job

▼▼

THE STORY OF JOB IS FOUND IN THE BOOK OF JOB IN THE OLD TES-
TAMENT of the Bible. His story begins with a happy Job, wealthy
and upright, but when God allows the Devil to test him, pain and
suffering enter his life.

Black people have long identified with Job. They can easily identify
with his suffering because of their experiences with suffering and oppression during slavery and afterward. They can easily identify with his
patience because many times in their experiences in America they have
had to be patient. They can easily identify with his faith because many
times in their experiences in America they have had to rely on faith to
inspire them not to give up.

The story of Job is dear to the heart of black people. It is mentioned in their songs, sermons, prayers, and everyday conversations.
It is also a source of strength and inspiration to them.

When I was a small boy growing up down South in the early
1960s, one of the favorite sermons of preachers back then was the
story of Job. It seemed like it was something about the story of Job
that made it special to black people back then. A sermon about Job

would arouse the church into a state of spiritual ecstasy like no other sermon. People would be shouting all over the church and praising God. They would be getting up and testifying to God's goodness, describing how good He had been to them. Some people in the church were working as laborers in cotton fields and as domestic servants, and they didn't have very much, but they were so thankful for the little bit that they had. They would thank God for having food to eat, clothes to wear, and a house to live in.

I have long enjoyed the story of Job whether in song or sermon, and I'm going to tell it to you. I'm going to tell it to you like the down-home black preachers of yesteryears would tell it to you. So, sit back and relax while I tell you the story of Job.

Back in the Bible days there lived in the land of Uz a wealthy and righteous man named Job. He owned thousands of sheep and camels and hundreds of oxen and asses; he had a large number of servants; and he was the father of seven sons and three daughters. Although he had much wealth, Job still feared God and avoided doing evil.

One day when God's sons were in his presence, Satan invited himself into the gathering. God asked Satan, where did you come from, Satan? Satan replied, "From going to and fro in the earth, and from walking up and down it."

God then told Satan about his good servant named Job, who was perfect, upright, and God-fearing. Satan told God that Job was like that because He had put a shield around him and would allow only good things to happen to him, but if He removed the shield and allowed bad things to happen to him, he would curse God to His face. God removed the shield from around Job and allowed Satan to test him.

Being allowed to test Job's faith in God pleased Satan. He was keenly aware that it was much easier to have faith in God when things were going well than when they weren't. He believed that when Job was tested with adversity, he would give up and curse God to His face.

One day while Job's children were feasting in the home of their oldest brother, a messenger came to Job and told him that robbers had stolen his oxen and asses and had killed the servants. Before the messenger could finish speaking, another messenger appeared and told Job that a fire had destroyed his sheep and the servants. Before this messenger could finish speaking, another one appeared and told Job that thieves had stolen his camels and had put the servants to the sword. But before this messenger could finish speaking, another one arrived with ghastly news. He told Job that a powerful wind had come up, and had destroyed the house his children were feasting in, and his children had been killed. Poor Job, in a matter of minutes, his whole life had fallen apart. He had lost property, servants, and even his children.

Despite his devastating losses, Job still maintained his faith in God and refused to denounce Him. Job's refusal to denounce God frustrated and angered Satan, and he devised another evil test to get Job to sin. This time Satan wanted to test Job by causing him to suffer physically instead of testing him by destroying his personal belongings. With this physically suffering test, Satan believed he could deliver the knockout blow to Job. In a conversation with God, Satan told God that if he were allowed to test Job by causing him to suffer physically, Job would fall apart and curse God to His face. God, believing in his faithful servant Job, allowed Satan to test him again.

Satan delivered Job a devastating blow, causing him to break out in nasty sore boils from the top of his head down to the bottom of his feet. Poor Job, suffering in pain and agony, took a piece of broken pottery and scraped his sores, after which "he sat down among the ashes." His wife saw him suffering and grieving, and in such bad shape, said to him, "Why do you continue to have faith in God when He lets you suffer like this? Curse God, and die."

But Job still had faith in God despite his awful suffering, and he refused to denounce God.

Meanwhile, three friends of Job, Eliphaz, Bildad, and Zophar "came to mourn with him and to comfort him." But when they saw Job's wretched condition, they were moved to tears, and for seven days and seven nights they sat with him in silence. Job began conversation by cursing the day he was born, which shocked his friends. They responded to his lamentations by telling him that if you sow wickedness you shall reap wickedness. They also told Job that he must be suffering because of his sins and he should repent to God. Job, however, told them that he was innocent of sin and had done nothing to cause his suffering. Finding no help from his friends, and disappointed with them, Job called upon God to speak directly to Him. Next, a young man named Elihu appeared on the scene. He was displeased with the arguments of Job and his friends. In his speech he offered the view that suffering may strengthen and clean a person. Next, God appeared to Job in a whirlwind. Job had requested a face-to-face meeting with God and now he had it. God, in a series of questions, showed Job His power and wisdom. "Job was humbled by God's power and wisdom," and realized that he was not qualified to question the will of God. Job asked God for forgiveness. In the end, God restored Job to wealth and happiness. He was given "twice as much as he had before." He was once again blessed with much property and a large family. Job enjoyed 140 years of prosperity and happiness before he died a very old man.

There are some similarities between Job's struggle in the Bible and black people's struggle during slavery. Satan tested Job like few men have ever been tested. During slavery black people were tested with the most dehumanizing slavery known to man and survived. Job suffered much pain during his ordeal. Black people also suffered much pain during slavery. When Job was tested by Satan, he was stripped of his children, servants, wealth, and health. When black people were tested by slavery, they were stripped of many things dear to their hearts.

During slavery just about everything was taken from the enslaved Africans. Slavers took them away from their home in Africa and brought them to America. The slavemasters took away their freedom, names, drums, languages, religions, and culture. Slave codes took away their right to read and write, so the light of knowledge couldn't enter their minds. Some slavemasters even took from their slaves the right to pray, causing them to have to pray in secret. Having taken away so much from the slaves, the slavemasters thought they had the slaves in a trap that they would never get out of. "But there was one thing the slavemasters couldn't take away from the slaves," and that was their faith in God. The slaves just kept on believing that they would be free one day. And lo and behold the Civil War broke out and freedom finally came. The faith the slaves had was more powerful than the slavemaster's whip; it was more powerful than the slavemaster; it was even more powerful than the institution of slavery itself.

ANALYSIS OF STORY

The story of Job revolved around Job's faith in God being tested by Satan. Satan told God that Job loved Him only because of the benefits that He gave him, and if they were taken away, he would curse God to His face. God allowed Satan to severely test Job twice, but thanks to Job's strong faith, he endured the pain and suffering of the tests and never cursed God. In the end, God restored Job to prosperity and happiness.

There is a lesson that can be learned from the story of Job and it is things that you hold dear can be taken away, sometimes due to circumstances beyond your control. Therefore, it doesn't pay to get too arrogant because you can be humbled.

The Lord Will Make a Way

▼▼

ANDRE FELT SAD AND DEPRESSED AS HE WALKED DOWN DELMAR AVENUE IN St. Louis on a warm fall day in October of 1993. He thought about the bad things that had happened in his life the past two years. First, his best friend Lamont had been fatally shot in a drive-by shooting. Next, he had quit his part-time job when the supervisor began complaining that he was lazy and a poor worker. Afterwards, he had dropped out of Westview Community College when he received two F's on his semester grade report. Finally, his heart had been broken when his girlfriend Linda quit him calling him a loser.

Because of the negative things that had happened to him the past two years, Andre's self-confidence was at an all-time low. He was beginning to doubt if he could succeed in life. He didn't know what he was going to do. The way things were going now, his future looked gloomy and bleak.

As Andre continued to walk down Delmar Avenue, he smelled the aroma of good food cooking. Suddenly, he realized that he was approaching Catherine's Restaurant, the home of the best soul food in St. Louis, Missouri. The food smelled so good to Andre that he decided to enter Catherine's Restaurant and eat dinner.

Andre entered the restaurant and ordered a catfish dinner. While he waited for the waitress to return with his food, he passed the time observing the people in the restaurant. He noticed that they were so busy eating and smacking their lips that they weren't talking at all. Andre thought to himself, "The food can't be that good."

After about ten minutes the waitress returned with his food, a plate heaped with fried catfish, spaghetti, potato salad, and bread. Andre ate and found the food delicious.

Suddenly, the quietness of the restaurant was broken by laughter. Andre looked over his left shoulder and saw that the noise was coming from the table where an old man and a young woman sat. They had finished eating and were now laughing, talking, and enjoying themselves. They seemed to be in such good spirits. Andre thought to himself, "What in the world could they be so happy about?"

As Andre continued to eat his dinner, the old man and young woman continued to laugh and talk. When he looked at them again, he noticed that they were looking at him and smiling. Andre smiled back at them and nodded his head.

The old man interpreted Andre's smile and nod as a sign of friendliness. He, therefore, came over to Andre's table with a warm smile on his face and said, "Hello, young man. How are you doing?"

Andre said, "Fine, Sir, and how are you doing?"

The old man replied, "I am doing very well, young man. Today is my ninetieth birthday. My granddaughter brought me over here to Catherine's Restaurant as part of my birthday celebration."

Andre said, "Happy birthday to you, Sir. You don't look over sixty years old."

The old man laughed and replied, "Thank you, young man. My name is Rev. Jasper Jones and the young lady with me is my grand daughter, Debra."

Andre said, "My name is Andre Walker."

Rev. Jasper Jones then told Andre that he and his granddaughter had observed him while he was eating, and he looked sad and depressed, and they wanted to join him at his table so they could engage him in conversation and cheer him up. Andre told the old preacher that it was okay for him and his granddaughter to join him at his table. The old preacher sat down at Andre's table and beckoned to his granddaughter to come and join them.

Rev. Jasper Jones and his granddaughter were very talkative, knowledgeable, and full of fun. They soon had Andre laughing and talking with them. The three talked about various subjects, from sports to politics to St. Louis gossip. After about an hour of talking about various subjects, the three changed the conversation to talking about themselves. Rev. Jasper Jones told Andre that he was no longer the pastor of a church, instead he was involved in volunteer community service, mostly helping young people get their lives together. Debra, his granddaughter, told Andre that she was a high school guidance-counselor. Andre said to them, "The reason I was looking so sad and depressed when you all were observing me is because I am going through some difficult times. I am unemployed; I have dropped out of college; and, worst of all, I am trying to recover from a broken heart. Linda, whom I was deeply in love with, quit me about three months ago."

Rev. Jasper Jones said, "Andre, I am sorry to hear about your misfortune. If you want me to, I will help you get your life back together."

Andre told him he would gladly accept his help. Rev. Jasper Jones then gave Andre his business card and told him to be sure to call him so he could help him.

Andre replied, " I sure will, Sir."

After Rev. Jasper Jones and his granddaughter tipped the waitress, they told Andre good-bye and said they were going home. As they were leaving, Andre thought to himself, "I sure enjoyed their company. It seems like I've known them all my life."

A week later, Andre called Rev. Jasper Jones. The old preacher was glad to hear from him. He suggested to Andre that all three of them get together again at Catherine's Restaurant, where they could eat some of that good soul food and talk. Andre told him that he looked forward to it. The date of their meeting was set for Friday of the following week.

When Andre arrived at Catherine's Restaurant, Rev. Jasper Jones and his granddaughter were already there. The three of them ordered fish dinners. After eating their delicious fish dinners, they began to talk seriously, opening up to each other, and rapping about their lives.

Debra said, "I was shy growing up and was uncomfortable meeting people. But I overcame my shyness by taking speech classes and learning to make friends with people. Now as a counselor, I enjoy meeting people and talking with them about their problems."

Andre said, "I am easily discouraged, and when adversity strikes me, I often give up. I've been like that all of my life. In elementary school I quit singing in the chorus because the kids laughed at my singing. In junior high school, I quit the football team because the coach became too demanding. About a year-and-a-half ago, I quit my job because the supervisor was complaining about my job performance. Last year, I quit attending college because I failed some courses. Right now I feel like a loser and my self-confidence is at an all-time low, and I don't know what I am going to do."

Rev. Jasper Jones said, "I understand how you feel Andre, but you can't give up. You need to ask God for strength. He will give you the strength to overcome your problems. You need to become a soldier on the battlefield, and fight to the end. The race is given neither to the swift nor the strong, but to the one who endures to the end. If you remain strong and don't give up, you can overcome your problems, and win in the end. I'm an old man, ninety years old, and I've been fighting on the battlefield a long time. In my life I've had many ups and downs, setbacks and failures, and sometimes I became discouraged but I never gave up, I always fought to the end. The Lord has been good to me. I was born in 1903 in Byhalia, Mississippi, a little town south of Memphis. My father and mother were sharecroppers and they had to struggle to raise me and my ten brothers and sisters to adulthood. I didn't go to school until I was twelve, but once I started school I made the most of it. I got as high as the fourth grade. Times were rough for black people back then. In 1921, at the age of eighteen, I married Sarah, my first wife. We began sharecropping with a man named Bill England. We worked hard planting, tilling, and harvesting the crops, but when it came 'settling time' in December, we made very little money. Most of the time 'Old Man Bill' would say we owed him for items we had bought during the year at his general store. He had the record book and he would keep us in debt by manipulating the figures. It was his figures against ours, and he had the law on his side, which made his figures correct. By 1926 I had had enough of sharecropping with 'Old Man Bill' and I told him my family and I were leaving his plantation."

Old Man Bill said to me, "Jasper, you can leave the plantation, but you can't take your mules or tools with you."

I looked him straight in his eyes and said, "When I move, I'm taking my mules, tools, and everything else I own with me."

After I told him that he just looked at me. I moved the next week and he didn't bother me. My family and I stayed in Mississippi one more year and in 1927 we left Mississippi and came north to St.

Louis. I supported my family here by preaching and working various jobs. I had a hard time supporting a wife and thirteen children but I did it. Yes, Sarah and I raised thirteen children to adulthood. We struggled at times but we made it. The Lord made a way for us. Sarah passed away fifteen years ago and I am now living with my second wife, Cora.

Andre said, "I am very impressed with you, Rev. Jasper Jones. You are quite a man. I want to be strong and confident like you."

Rev. Jasper Jones said, "Andre, you can overcome your problems but you will have to quit giving up when things get difficult. You have to be a fighter to the end. If you don't give up during the night, you will be able to see the bright sunshine of day. If you believe in God, He will make a way for you. When things get difficult, just keep on believing and trusting in the Lord, and He will make a way for you. You can overcome your problems Andre, if you try hard enough. Remember, whatever you do, give it your very best effort and it will pay off."

Andre watched as Rev. Jasper Jones and his granddaughter left the restaurant. He thought to himself, "I am in awe of this old preacher. He is ninety years old but he walks and looks like he is sixty years old. His words have really inspired me. Just being in his presence has made me feel more confident. I believe now that if I try hard enough, I can overcome all of my problems."

When Andre got home, he told his mother about Rev. Jasper Jones and how his encouraging words had inspired him to the point that he now felt like he could overcome all of his problems. His mother was happy for him. She was aware of all of his problems and had been hoping that he would find the strength to try to get his life back together.

Armed with increased self-confidence, Andre began looking for a job. He looked for weeks and finally found a part-time job as a shoe salesman in a department store. Although it didn't pay very much, Andre saw it as a means to an end.

Andre took a positive attitude to his new job as a shoe salesman at Brown's Department Store. He always arrived at work on time and was very courteous to the customers. His supervisor was impressed with his job performance. Within three months, he had received a nice little raise.

Andre's success on the job was a big psychological boost to him. He began to think that his success on the job meant that he could now be successful in college. He, therefore, reenrolled in Westview Community College to complete an associate degree in accounting.

This time Andre brought a more serious attitude to college with him. Instead of spending hours in the student union socializing with his friends, he spent hours in the library studying and doing his homework. His commitment to school paid off at the end of the fall semester in the form of A's and B's. Andre was very encouraged by his good grades. They were the best that he had ever made in school.

Andre started the spring semester of 1995 at Westview with a high degree of self-confidence. He was determined to continue his good work in the classroom. He wanted to do as well the spring semester as he had done the fall semester.

When Andre attended the first meeting of his math class, he saw a young lady that really looked good to him. She was tall, shapely, and very attractive. On the way home from school that night, all Andre could think about was the dark beauty he had seen in class. He thought to himself, "I'm going to get acquainted with her at the next class meeting."

However, at the next class meeting Andre didn't say a word to her. He just couldn't build up the nerve to approach her. It wasn't until the fourth class meeting that he finally built up the nerve to introduce himself to her and get acquainted with her. He learned that her name was Michelle Brown, she was majoring in math, she was twenty years old and single, and had broken up with her boyfriend a few months ago.

Now that Andre had introduced himself to Michelle, he began to talk to her after each class meeting. But he still couldn't build up the nerve to tell her how much he liked her and ask her for a date. One day at work he decided to tell Rev. Jasper Jones, his mentor, about his problem. He, therefore, called him on the telephone. The old preacher was glad to hear his voice. When he told him about his situation with Michelle, the old preacher told him not to be shy about telling the young lady how he felt about her and to ask her for a date. Rev. Jasper Jones then said to Andre, "Young man, you have nothing to lose if the young lady says no and everything to gain if she says yes. Go for it. Think of it this way, if she rejects you she has lost a good man; and furthermore, if you don't catch this fish, there are still plenty of nice fish in the great, big sea that have never been caught."

Andre thanked Rev. Jasper Jones for his advice. His words had filled him with confidence. Andre thought to himself, "At the next class meeting I'm going to tell Michelle how much I like her and then I'm going to ask her for a date."

Andre went to the next math class with Michelle on his mind. When the class was over, he as usual, began talking to her. During the conversation he told her how pretty he thought she was. Andre's compliment surprised Michelle, she hadn't expected that from him, but she smiled and said, "Thank you, Andre."

Andre then told Michelle how much he liked her and that he would like very much to take her to the movies Saturday night. To Andre's surprise and delight, she answered, "Sure, we can go to the movies Saturday night."

Andre felt ten feet tall as he dressed to take Michelle to the movies. His wish had finally come true. He made sure that he was looking his best. He wanted to make a good impression on her. He also made sure that his car was shined and looking good. When he arrived at Michelle's house, she introduced him to her family. After the introduction, Andre thought to himself, "The Browns seem to be a nice family."

Andre and Michelle enjoyed the movie at the theater. After the movie Andre took Michelle back to her house, where they chatted for awhile. When Andre left for home, Michelle's grandmother asked her, "Michelle, how did your date with Andre go tonight?"

Michelle answered, "I enjoyed the movie but Andre is kind of boring and dull, also he's not that handsome. You know, I am attracted to guys who are handsome, flashy, and have a smooth rap."

Her grandmother said, "Michelle, don't be so quick to judge the book by its cover. A book may have a very attractive cover but it might be boring when you read it, whereas a book with a plain cover might turn out to be a good book when you read it. Back in the 1960s, before your time, the singing group, The Temptations, used to sing a song called 'Beauty Is Only Skin Deep,' which means a person can be ugly on the outside but beautiful on the inside and vice versa. What I am trying to say, Michelle, is Andre might not be flashy and good-looking, but he may possess good qualities such as honesty, kindness, patience, compassion, and intelligence. Give him a chance; he may turn out to be a diamond in the rough. Michelle, your last boyfriend, Maurice, was flashy and handsome, but he turned out to be a slickster. He used and mistreated you. And your boyfriend before him, Charles, was a carbon copy of Maurice. You are attracted to these same types of men who don't mean you any good. I have been praying for the Lord to send you a good man. Andre may be the one; he seems like a nice young man. You know the Lord sometimes works in mysterious ways."

Michelle replied, "Grandmother, Andre just isn't my type, but I will go out with him one more time, and if he is still boring and dull on the second date, I won't go out with him anymore. That will be it."

Andre saw Michelle at the next math class meeting. He talked to her after class and asked her could he take her out to dinner Friday evening. Michelle hesitated at first and started to say no, but she changed her mind at the last moment and said, "Yes, I will go to dinner with you Andre."

When Friday evening came they went to Catherine's Restaurant for dinner. Michelle found the food delicious. She also enjoyed her evening with Andre. He was more lively and interesting than last time, and he even complimented her on how good she looked. She even saw Andre's sense of humor for the first time. He told her about a funny incident that had happened on his job, which made her burst her sides laughing.

After Andre brought Michelle home, she tried to watch television, but it was hard for her to concentrate on the picture because her mind kept wandering off to thoughts about the dinner she had had with Andre. She had enjoyed herself with him. She thought to herself, "Andre is a very nice guy. He has a good outlook on life, and he is positive. I'm starting to like him. I'm going to date him again."

Andre and Michelle continued to date the rest of the year. They had a wonderful time going to movies, concerts, baseball games, plays, and parties. They especially enjoyed their romantic hand-in-hand walks in Forest Park. By the time Christmas came Andre had fallen deeply in love with Michelle. But on the other hand, he wasn't sure she felt the same way about him. He knew she liked him but he wasn't sure about the love. He also knew that his feelings were stronger for her than her feelings were for him.

When January of 1996 arrived, it marked one year that Andre

and Michelle had been dating. They were both still attending Westview Community College and were planning on graduating in May.

The month of February came in with a bang and you could feel the romance in the air. Andre was now so much in love with Michelle that he decided to write her a poem for Valentine's Day. It took him a while to write the poem but when he finished it, he liked it. He then mailed it to Michelle along with some other items.

Meanwhile, Michelle looked in many different stores before she finally found the perfect Valentine card for Andre. It described to a tee her feelings for him. She signed it and mailed it to him.

On Valentine's Day Michelle received a package from Andre. It contained roses, a box of candy, and a fancy letter. She opened the letter, and to her surprise, it contained a homemade Valentine card, which was very beautiful. She opened the card and was even more surprised when she saw that he had written her a poem entitled "I Love You." It read:

I LOVE YOU

I have a little secret
That I want you to hear
I love you more than I've ever
Loved anyone else, my dear.

My love for you
Is so strong
That you can
Do no wrong.

If the moon falls from the
Sky and the sun turns blue,

I will still keep
On loving you.

If walls could talk and if
Cupid's arrow could sing,
They would both tell you that my
Love for you is the real thing.

You are the beautiful
Queen of the Nile.
My heart skips a beat
Each time I see you smile.

If I couldn't see you,
I don't know what I would do.
Just the sight of you
Chills me through and through.

If you were a ship
Far out on the sea,
I would wish and wish that
You would sail home to me.

So, my beautiful queen
If you love me too
It will make me so happy
That I won't know what to do.

Robert L. Bradley, July, 1997

Michelle enjoyed reading Andre's poem. She thought it was a
beautiful expression of his love for her. She thought to herself, "Al-

though Andre is in love with me, I still haven't fallen in love with him yet. However, I care a lot about him. It takes me a while to fall in love but when I do, my love is very strong."

In April Andre told Michelle that his job was sending him out of town for two weeks. While he was out of town Michelle really missed him. She felt so lonely without him around that she didn't know what to do. She found herself just sitting around waiting for him to return. And while she was sitting around waiting for him to return it suddenly hit her that the reason she missed him so much was because she was in love with him. When Andre returned, Michelle sent him a card. It read, "Andre, I missed you so much while you were gone. Your absence made me realize that I am in love with you. You are the most caring person I have ever known. You make me feel like a queen. I wouldn't trade you for all the men in the world. I love you so very much. I love you so much that words can not adequately express how much I love you."

Andre was very happy after reading Michelle's card. His beautiful Queen was now finally in love with him. He was no longer in love alone.

In May Andre and Michelle graduated from Westview Community College. Andre received an associate degree in accounting and Michelle received an associate degree in math. Their families and friends were so proud of them. Andre's mother Clara was especially proud of him. After he received his diploma, she gave him a big, affectionate hug and said, "Andre, you did it. I told you that you could do it."

Andre's mentor, Rev. Jasper Jones, also attended the graduation and he was very happy for Andre. He said, "Andre, you have come such a long way. I am so happy for you. You have completely turned your life around. When I first met you nearly three years ago at Catherine's Restaurant, you were very despondent; you had quit your job, you had dropped out of college, and you were suffering from a broken heart. Now you have a job, a degree, and a beautiful young lady who loves you. God has been good to you. He has made a way for you. Your accomplishments are a testimony to what you can do if you work hard, believe in yourself, and don't give up."

In September Andre and Michelle enrolled in Douglass University to continue their education. Andre sought a bachelor's degree in accounting and Michelle sought a bachelor's degree in math. They both planned to graduate within three years. Time moved fast and by the end of May 1998, they had successfully completed two years of study at Douglass University with one year left to go. They had done this despite holding down part-time jobs. In August they happily announced that they were going to get married. The wedding was set for the first Saturday in August the next year, 1999.

Andre and Michelle continued their hard work at Douglass University and graduated in May of 1999. Andre received a bachelor's degree in accounting and Michelle received a bachelor's degree in math. Within a month they both had new jobs. Andre was hired as an accountant by a bank and Michelle was hired as a computer programmer by an insurance company.

In early August, Andre's older brother Joe Jr. arrived in St. Louis from Seattle, Washington for the wedding. He was greeted very warmly by his mother Clara, his sister Terri, and his little brother Andre. They were glad to see him. That night at the dinner table he congratulated Andre for turning his life around. He said to him, "Andre, I am so happy that you were able to graduate from college and get a good job. I was worried about you when Mama told me that you had quit your job and had dropped out of college. For awhile I thought you might give up trying to make it and start self-destructing out of frustration, turning to crime and drugs. But thanks to the inspirational words of Rev. Jasper Jones, you hung in there and didn't give up. Mama told me he is a young ninety-five years old. I am anxious to meet him; he must be some kind of man."

When Joe Jr., met Michelle for the first time the next day, he was overwhelmed by her charm and beauty. He said to Andre, "Man, you didn't tell me you were going to marry a queen. Michelle looks and acts like a queen. You have done all right for yourself, Little Brother."

On August 6, 1999, Andre Walker and Michelle Brown were united in holy matrimony before a packed church. They were married by Andre's mentor, Rev. Jasper Jones. Michelle's maid of honor was her best friend, Ann. Andre's best man was his brother, Joe Jr.

After the wedding ceremony, Andre and Michelle were all smiles. They were finally husband and wife. Andre felt like the most blessed man in the world, having married his dream lady.

As Andre and Michelle walked to the waiting limousine, Andre thought to himself, "The Lord has really blessed me. I have come a long way since the fall of 1993 when I was at such a low point that I had quit believing in myself. Now, I believe in myself. If adversity gets in my way, I won't give up; instead I will struggle against it because I believe I can overcome it. I am now a strong and courageous soldier on the battlefield; I will fight to the end. The Lord has made a way for me."

ANALYSIS OF STORY

This story "The Lord Will Make a Way" illustrates that God has given you the power within yourself to overcome your problems if you struggle against your problems to the end, rather than give up. Andre Walker had reached a low point in his life. He had dropped out of college; he had lost his best friend, his job, and his girlfriend; and worst of all, he had lost his self-confidence. He no longer believed in himself. But when he heard Rev. Jasper Jones' inspiring and encouraging words, he decided to struggle to overcome his problems instead of giving up. And in the end he overcame his problems and turned his life around. He looked for a job and found one. He returned to college and graduated. He built up the nerve to woo attractive Michelle Brown and eventually captured her love. And in Rev. Jasper Jones he replaced the best friend that he had lost in a drive-by shooting. So, in the final analysis, the Lord made a way for Andre because he believed that the Lord would.

Look on the Bright Side

▼▼▼

DURING THE SEASONS OF A YEAR THERE WILL BE DAYS THAT ARE DARK AND gloomy, but eventually the sun will shine. The same thing is true for a person's life. A man will have dark and gloomy days but eventually God will send some bright sunshine into his life. However, if the man gives up during the dark and gloomy days, he will never see the days that will be sunny and bright.

I have long believed in the reality of a bright side, and if I didn't give up, I would eventually see it. Believing this has helped me to accomplish goals over the years. It has also enabled me to successfully deal with adversity.

The expression "look on the bright side" has inspired me to create a story entitled "Look on the Bright Side," which deals with the difficulties a teenager encounters while trying to play basketball for his high school team.

Freshman Larry McNeil was very excited as he entered the gym for basketball practice. This was the day Coach Thomas would announce the players who had made Howard High's varsity basketball team and, of course, Larry expected to be one of them.

As usual, Coach Thomas drove the players hard during the basketball practice. They did exercises, they ran sprints, they worked on fundamentals, and finally they played a scrimmage basketball game to help determine the last cuts.

After the scrimmage game, Coach Thomas told the players to gather around him so he could announce the players who had made his varsity basketball team. Larry listened carefully as Coach Thomas called off the names of the players who had made the team, but he didn't hear his name called. Larry couldn't believe that his name hadn't been called! Coach Thomas must have made some kind of mistake when he didn't call his name. Suddenly, it dawned on him that he hadn't made the team; he had been cut. Larry just couldn't believe it. He was in a state of shock. He knew that he had better basketball skills than some of the players who had made the team.

When Larry came home from basketball practice, his mother could sense that he was upset about something. She asked him, "Larry, what's wrong?"

Larry answered sadly, "Mama, I didn't make the varsity basketball team. Coach Thomas cut me today. But I should have made it because I am better than some of the players he kept."

His mother said, "Larry, I am sorry to hear that you didn't make the team but you will just have to try harder next year."

Larry replied, "Mama, there won't be a next year because I will never go out for Coach Thomas' basketball team again. He isn't fair; he keeps the players he likes and cuts the players he doesn't like."

His mother said, "Larry, I am not sure about that, from what I have heard, Coach Thomas is a fair but very demanding coach."

Larry didn't respond to his mother's comments about Coach Thomas. Instead, he sat at the table and began to slowly eat his food. While he was eating his food, his father walked into the house from work. His father knew by the look on his face that he was upset about something. His father asked, "Larry, why are you so quiet this evening? Normally, when I walk into the house you begin laughing and talking with me."

Larry replied, "Daddy, Coach Thomas cut me today. He didn't think I was good enough to make his basketball team."

His father said, "What? Larry, you are telling me you didn't make Coach Thomas' basketball team, as good as you can shoot and handle the ball? You got to be kidding me!"

Larry said, "That's right, Daddy, I didn't make the team but I am better than some of the players who made it."

His father, getting somewhat emotional, said, "I'm going to call Coach Thomas on the telephone right now, have a little talk with him, and find out why he cut you today."

Larry's father called Coach Thomas and asked him why his son, Larry McNeil, didn't make his team, even though he had better skills than some of the players who had made it. Coach Thomas responded, "Yes, Mr. McNeil, your son does have better basketball skills than some of the players who made my team, but he doesn't like to play defense. In order for a player to make my team, he has to commit himself to playing good defense. My team's offense feeds off of its defense. I like for my players to hustle on defense the entire time they are on the court. Your son is a good shooter and ball handler but he needs to improve his defense and attitude to make my team. However, he is only a freshman, and if he improves these two areas, he has an excellent chance of making my team next year. He will be a sophomore then."

Larry's father said, "Thanks, Coach Thomas, for explaining to me why my son didn't make your basketball team. When he tries out for your team next year, I will make sure he has improved in the areas you talked about."

After his father got off the telephone, Larry said to him, "Daddy, you don't have to worry about me making the basketball team next year. I'll never try out for Coach Thomas' basketball team again. I am through with basketball and Coach Thomas too."

Larry's father replied, "Son, life isn't always easy and there will be times when trouble gets in your way, but you can't give up. I want you to work hard to improve your weaknesses in basketball. You need to improve your defense and your attitude. You are a good shooter and ball handler but you don't like to play defense. I want you to work hard to improve your defense. Try out for Coach Thomas' basketball team next year and give it your best shot. I believe if you work hard to improve your game, you will be an outstanding basketball player. You have height, quickness, and jumping ability. I believe there is a bright side for you in basketball if you don't give up. But if you give up, you will never see the bright side. You need to look on the bright side of things. It will inspire you not to give up when faced with adversity."

Larry said, "Daddy, thanks a million for your encouraging words. You have inspired me to change my mind about basketball. Instead of quitting, I am going to work hard to improve my defense and attitude. Next year I'm trying out again for Coach Thomas' basketball team, and I'm going to make it."

In order to improve Larry's game, his father decided to let him play basketball on a YMCA team rather than on Howard High's junior varsity team. The reason for this move was the YMCA team was coached by a man who specialized in teaching young players how to improve their basketball game.

The name of the YMCA team that Larry played on was called the Northside Hornets. Its coach, Patrick Collins, a defensive specialist, had an eye for evaluating a player's potential. He told Larry that he had the potential to be an outstanding basketball player if he worked hard at improving his game. Coach Collins took a liking to

Larry and was able to motivate him to work hard. Coach Collin's team played an up tempo game, combined with a pressing defense. Larry's game thrived under the tutelage of Coach Collins; his skills improved tremendously, especially his defense. By the end of the season, Larry had become a good all-around basketball player. His team the Northside Hornets won first place in the league they played in.

When Larry tried out for the Howard High varsity basketball team his sophomore year, he was determined to make it. From day one, he showed Coach Thomas lots of hustle on defense. He stole the ball from careless dribblers, he dived for loose balls, and he intercepted poorly thrown passes. He also showed Coach Thomas that he was skilled at shooting, dribbling, and passing. Coach Thomas was impressed with Larry's all-around-game. He couldn't believe that his game had improved so much in only a year. He also was impressed with his good attitude. Larry not only made Coach Thomas' varsity team; he made the starting five as well.

Larry McNeil had a fine year as a sophomore at Howard High School in St. Louis, Missouri. The 6 foot, 2 inch guard led his team in scoring with a 20.0 point average and in steals with 3 per game. His smooth and exciting play won him praise from teammates, fans, opponents, and Coach Thomas. He became the focus of much attention in the St. Louis area. His brilliant all-around-play enabled the Howard High Magicians to go all the way to the semi-finals of the state tournament before losing to the eventual state champion.

Larry's parents were very proud of his sophomore year accomplishments in basketball. They were especially proud of how he had bounced back from being cut his freshman year. They had also given him much support during the year, having attended every game he had played.

When Larry returned to school for his junior year, everyone

asked him how good the 1997-98 basketball team was going to be. Larry told them he thought the team would be good enough to win the state tournament. Coach Thomas also told people that he thought the team would be good enough to win the state championship with most of the players returning from last year's team.

The thought of winning a state championship created much excitement around Howard High the fall of 1997. The excitement turned to gloom, however, when word spread that star basketball player Larry McNeil had received three F's on his report card and was having academic problems. The situation was that he couldn't play basketball when the season opened, but if he improved his grade point average, he would be eligible to play in January.

Larry felt very bad about his academic problems. He had let the fame from being a basketball star swell his head and distract him from doing his schoolwork. Now he had to raise his grade point average to a 2.00, or he wouldn't be allowed to play basketball in January. To accomplish this, he had to make at least three A's and three B's on his next grade report.

Larry told his parents about his academic problems and that he was ineligible to play on the basketball team until he improved his grades. They were very disappointed with his poor classroom performance but were sympathetic to his problems. Larry also told them about all the pressure he was under to raise his grade point average to a 2.00 so he could be eligible to play basketball in January. After Larry had finished speaking, his father asked, "Son, what grades do you have to make in order to raise your grade point average to a 2.00 on your next grade report?"

Larry answered, "Daddy, I have to make at least three A's and three B's to raise my grade point average to a 2.00."

His father said, "Larry, you can do it if you give it your best effort."

The next day at the supper table Larry looked very sad. His father asked him, "Larry, why are you looking so sad today?"

Larry answered, "Daddy, when my friends and I were eating lunch in the cafeteria today, I overheard some students laughing and snickering, and saying unkind things about me. One student in particular was very hard on me. He said, 'Larry McNeil is too dumb to improve his grades, how can he make A's and B's when he can't make C's, there is no way he will be eligible to play basketball in January? We might as well kiss our chance at a state championship good-bye.'"

Larry's father said, "Son, you need to learn to ignore people's unkind words and not let them bother you."

Larry replied, "Daddy, it isn't easy to ignore the unkind words of those students. Their unkind words hurt me and shook my confidence. I have decided to quit basketball because there is no way I can make three A's and three B's on my next grade report."

Larry's father said, "Son, if you give up now because things have gotten difficult, you will be giving up to adversity all of your life. Hang in there; don't quit. A quitter never wins and a winner never quits. I believe there is a bright side for you in basketball, but if you give up, you will never see it. Don't give up this easy. You can make those three A's and three B's if you try hard enough."

Larry replied, "Okay, Daddy, I'm not going to quit; I'm going to try my best to make those good grades. Also, I'm going to let those students' negative comments about my academic problems serve as a motivating force. I'm going to show them something."

True to his word, Larry tried his very best to improve his grades. He made sure he did all of his homework everyday, he spent hours reading in the public library to enhance his knowledge, and he studied harder for his tests than he had ever studied in his life. In short, he gave a supreme effort to overcome his academic problems.

When report card day finally arrived in January, Larry was feeling apprehensive as he walked to school that morning. He hoped that his report card would show three A's and three B's. But to his surprise when he opened his report card that evening, he saw all A's. Larry was so surprised by the straight A's that he was speechless, he just stared at the report card in disbelief, then he shouted with uncontrollable happiness, "I am eligible to play on the basketball team! I am eligible to play on the basketball team!"

He was so excited that his girlfriend Angie and other students had to calm him down. They had never seen him that excited before.

Larry rejoined the Howard High basketball team in mid-January. Coach Thomas and his teammates were very happy to see him return. They had struggled somewhat without him, having posted a 10-6 record. In his first game back, before an overflow crowd in the home gym, Larry scored 33 points, made 4 steals, and handed out 5 assists in a 90-75 win over a good Wilson High team. Inspired by Larry's leadership and great all-around play, the Howard High Magicians won game after game, including wins over the following teams, a hard fought 69-62 victory over arch rival St. Anthony, a close 66-63 win over North High to capture the tough St. Louis Public High League crown, and an even closer 81-80 win over previously undefeated Dubois High in the district tournament finals.

After winning the district tournament, the Howard High Magicians continued their winning ways and advanced to the Missouri 4A state championship game. In this championship game they faced the powerful Woodson High Golden Lions of the Kansas City Public High League, who were undefeated at 33-0.

In the Howard High Magicians-Woodson High Golden Lions match up, it was the quickness of the Magicians against the power and height of the Golden Lions. The game started with Woodson

High taking a 20-12 lead after the first quarter, but by halftime the lighting quick Magicians had evened the score at 36 apiece, thanks to their pressing defense and potent fast-break. Larry McNeil led all scorers at half time with 12 points. In the third quarter Larry McNeil had the crowd "oohing and ahing" with his fancy passes and pretty fade-away jump shots that hit nothing but the bottom of the net. After three quarters the Magicians led the Golden Lions by one, 56 to 55. The fourth quarter began with the Woodson High Golden Lions going on an 8-0 run and taking a 63-56 lead over the Howard High Magicians, then the Magicians put on a furious rally, and with four minutes left in the game, they led Woodson High by 4 points, 70 to 66. The next two trips down the court neither team scored, then the unexpected happened, Larry McNeil went up high for a rebound and came down hard on a Woodson High player's foot, which severely injured his ankle and he had to be carried from the court. With their star player injured and out of the game, the Howard High Magicians weren't the same team. They put up a gallant effort against the powerful Woodson High Golden Lions the last three minutes but were beaten 76 to 74. After the game many people said that if Larry McNeil hadn't got injured, Howard High would have won the state championship.

Larry McNeil finished the championship game against Woodson High with 29 points, 6 rebounds, 5 assists, and 3 steals. He was named to the all-tournament team.

When Larry returned home to St. Louis from the state tournament, his father took him to the family doctor and had his swollen foot examined. It turned out that he had a broken bone in his foot rather than a severely sprained ankle, which would take months to heal. Larry was undaunted, however, by his foot injury. He said, "Daddy, I bounced back from being cut by Coach Thomas, I bounced back from academic problems, and I'm going to come back from this foot injury. I believe that there is a bright side for me in basketball if I don't give up. From now on, I'm going to look on the bright side of things and I'm not going to let anyone or anything turn me around."

Larry's foot injury healed perfectly and by late October, he was ready to participate in Coach Thomas' grueling basketball practices. Coach Thomas drove his players hard, because he wanted them to be ready for the upcoming basketball season. He believed that if his team was properly prepared, it was capable of taking the state crown away from powerful Woodson High of Kansas City.

Larry McNeil now entered his senior year at Howard High. He was 6-5 and weighed 200 lbs. He was also an excellent all-around-player. He could do it all: shoot, defend, handle the ball, rebound, pass, and jump. What he wanted most of all, however, was to be part of a state championship team.

The Howard High Magicians began their season in mid-November in a prestigious tournament in Springfield, Missouri. In their first game, they rolled over Wonder High 100 to 68; in their second game, they crushed Johnson High 105 to 65; and in the championship game, they beat a strong Liberty City High team 70 to 61. In the Springfield tournament, Larry McNeil was the talk of the town as he dazzled fans with his slam-dunks, deadly outside shooting, and no-look passes. The Howard High Magicians won the remainder of their games in November. They also won all of their games in December and January. In early February the 20-0 Magicians traveled to Chicago to play traditional powerhouse Booker T. Washington High, undefeated at 23-0. The game was close all the way and very exciting. With two seconds left in the game Larry McNeil was fouled attempting a jump shot, he hit both pressure-filled free throws, which gave the Magicians a close 68-67 win over Chicago's Booker T. Washington High. The Magicians won their next five games and finished the regular season at 26-0. In addition to being undefeated, the Magicians were also the St. Louis Public High League champs for the third year in a row.

The Howard High Magicians won the district tournament but it wasn't easy. An overflow crowd watched them come from behind and beat tough rival Dubois High 75 to 70. In this district championship game, sharp-shooting Larry McNeil had 30 points, 6 rebounds, 3 steals, and 4 assists.

After winning their first three games of the state tournament, the Magicians once again faced powerful Woodson High of Kansas City for the state championship.

The Howard High-Woodson High rematch had basketball fans and sportswriters excited all over the state. Some fans predicted Woodson High to repeat as state champions. They said that there was no way Howard High could beat powerful Woodson High, whose three frontline players were all 6-8. Some sportswriters also said that there was no way Howard High could beat Woodson High, which was riding a 65 game win streak. On the other hand, there were some fans and sportswriters who believed the Magicians could beat Woodson High because of their team speed and quickness and great player Larry McNeil, who had the ability to make his teammates better.

The state championship game was played before a standing room only crowd at the Hearnes Center in Columbia, Missouri. The first quarter was action-packed as both teams battled to a 16-16 tie. In the second quarter, Larry McNeil got hot, putting on an awesome display of deadly outside shooting, which enabled his team to grab a 40-32 half time lead. The Woodson High Golden Lions came out the third quarter all fired up and hustling all over the court. By the end of the third quarter, they had turned an 8-point deficit into an 8-point lead, 54 to 46. On the other hand, in the third quarter, the Magicians played poorly and were ice cold from the field, scoring only 6 points on free throws, and were unable to stop the powerful inside game of Woodson High. The fourth quarter began with Woodson High taking the ball inside and scoring at will. With six minutes left in the game, they led the Howard High Magicians 62 to 48. Sensing his team was about to fall apart, Coach Thomas called a time out. In the time out he gave the Howard High Magicians a very inspiring pep talk, telling them they could still win the game even though they were 14 points down with only six minutes left on the clock. He also told them to go into their full court press and pressure the ball all over the court. Inspired by Coach Thomas' encouraging words, the Magicians came back onto the court with fire in their eyes. Larry McNeil immediately stole the ball, dribbled the length of the basketball court, and jammed home a monster dunk, which electrified his teammates and sent the Magician fans into a frenzy. The comeback was on, the Magicians tenacious full court press forced the Woodson High players into numerous turnovers which were quickly turned into points by the speedy Magician players. With one minute left in the game, the Howard High Magicians had erased a 14 point deficit and were leading Woodson High by two points, 66 to 64. Not to be denied, however, Woodson High came back to take a 68 to 66 lead with eighteen seconds left in the game. Howard High then brought the ball up the court but was called for a walking violation while trying to run a play to free Larry McNeil for a shot. The costly turnover gave the ball back to the Woodson High Golden Lions. The Golden Lions now just had to run eight seconds off the clock and the game was theirs. It looked like Howard High had lost again in the championship game, trailing Woodson High by two points with only eight seconds left in the game. However, the Magicians' full court press was so tenacious that Woodson High was unable to inbound the ball and was called for a time violation. The ball now belonged to the Howard High Magicians, and it was under their basket. They had eight seconds left on the clock to try to win the basketball game or tie it up. The ball was inbounded to Larry McNeil who did a behind the back dribble that so confused his defender that he fell to the floor. Larry McNeil then launched a long jumper from behind the three -point line that swished the net as the buzzer sounded, ending the game.

Larry's game winning three point shot caused pandemonium to break loose in the Hearnes Center. Hundreds of raving fans poured onto the court screaming, "We did it! We did it! We beat Woodson High for the state championship!" The fans were in such a frenzied state that it took fifteen minutes to restore order in the sports arena.

The Howard High Magicians thrilling come from behind victory over Woodson High gave them the Missouri 4A state championship for the first time. In the 69 to 68 win over Woodson High Larry McNeil had an excellent game. He poured in 28 points, handed out 5 assists, grabbed 7 rebounds, and had 3 steals. For his great effort he was named the tournament's MVP.

Howard High's basketball players showed a lot of heart and determination in winning the state championship. The school, and especially Coach Thomas, was so proud of them. For weeks after the championship game, students around Howard High talked of little else but Larry McNeil's heroic game winning shot.

One evening in late April, Larry's father said to him, "Son, you have worked very hard this school year, both athletically and academically, and it has paid off. You have been selected all- metro, all-state, and all-American in high school basketball. You have also made the honor roll every quarter this school year. Congratulations for being such a fine scholar-athlete. I am so proud of you!"

Larry replied, "Thanks, Daddy, for your nice comments about

me, but without your encouragement and inspiring words, I wouldn't be an honor student and a high school all-American basketball player, instead I would be a quitter. You told me that you believed there was a bright side for me in basketball if I worked hard and didn't give up. Well, I have worked hard and didn't give up and, therefore, I have seen that bright side in basketball."

Larry's father said, "Larry, I know you are aware that some people are saying that you are good enough right now to play pro basketball and you should enter the NBA's draft in June. However, I hope you decide to attend college this fall."

Larry replied, "Daddy, I have already decided to attend college this fall, I don't think I am quite ready for the NBA right now. Those pro basketball players are good. When I get to their level, I want to be able to successfully compete against them."

Larry's father said, "Son, I am so happy that you have made the decision to attend college this fall. Getting a college education is very important because you will always have a degree to fall back on just in case pro ball doesn't work out the way you hope it will. However, I believe you will make a good pro when the time comes for you to play at that level. I feel very confident about your future. I believe you will be very successful in life because of your positive attitude."

Larry replied, "Daddy, I believe I am going to be successful in life too, because I am going to always look on the bright side of things. I am not going to let anyone or anything make me give up."

ANALYSIS OF STORY

This story "Look on the Bright Side" illustrates the importance of remaining positive when faced with adversity. Teenage basketball player, Larry McNeil, was tested by adversity while trying to play basketball for his high school team. Faced with adversity, he wanted to give up a couple of times. He wanted to give up when he failed to make the varsity basketball team his freshman year. He also wanted to give up when he encountered academic problems his junior year. However, his father encouraged him not to give up both times. In the final analysis, Larry McNeil overcame all of his difficulties and lead his high school team his senior year to the state championship, which brought him much fame and recognition.

The Power of Prayer

▼▼▼

ON A COLD WINTER DAY IN NASHVILLE, TENNESSEE, FEBRUARY OF 1975, Mrs. Mitchell was cooking dinner when her fifteen year old daughter, Shelia, rushed into the house from school with a big smile on her face. Observing Shelia's big smile, Mrs. Mitchell asked, "Shelia, why are you so happy this evening?"

Sheila answered, "Mama, guess what! I've been chosen by my chorus teacher to play the role of singer Mahalia Jackson in a school play next week celebrating Black History Month. I'm so excited about it! You know how much I love to sing. In the play, I'm going to sing some of the songs that made Mahalia Jackson famous."

Mrs. Mitchell said, "That's wonderful Shelia. I'm looking forward to listening to you sing some of Mahalia Jackson's songs. She was one of my favorite singers."

The play celebrating Black History Month was held in the school auditorium, which was filled to capacity. In the play, Shelia sang three of Mahalia Jackson's favorite songs. The audience thoroughly enjoyed her rendition of the song "Move on up a Little Higher." Some people in the audience were moved to tears when

Shelia sang the song "There's Not a Friend like Jesus." But when she sang the song "Amazing Grace" the whole audience came alive. People rocked, they hollered, and they got up out of their seats. When Shelia finished singing "Amazing Grace", she was given a standing ovation by the audience.

After the play, Shelia was congratulated by friends, fellow students, teachers, and parents. They said, "Shelia, we didn't know you had such a beautiful singing voice. Your singing of Mahalia Jackson's songs was outstanding. Mahalia Jackson couldn't have sung those songs any better."

Sheila's outstanding performance in the play made her mother so proud. Mrs. Mitchell said to Sheila, "Baby, you were just great tonight. You sang like a seasoned professional. I am so proud of you. All of your hard work practicing your singing voice the last ten years has paid off."

Sheila replied, "Yes, mama, it sure has. I am only fifteen years old and a sophomore in high school, but I have been singing in our church since I was five years old."

Sheila continued to sing in her church and in other churches in the metropolitan Nashville area. Her beautiful solos were a joy to hear. They had people all over the city saying, "That girl can really sing! Someday she is going to be a famous singer."

After Sheila graduated from high school in 1977, she began singing gospel professionally. At first she just sang in the metropolitan Nashville area, but her rising popularity soon caught the ears of gospel promoters across the nation, and they began contacting her and booking her for gospel concerts all over the United States. Wherever she sang: Memphis, Atlanta, Detroit, Dallas, or Baltimore, people flocked to listen to her magnificent singing voice. At these gospel concerts, she sang "unforgettable favorites" such as "Old Ship of Zion," "The Lord Will Make a Way Somehow," "A Mother Loves

Her Children," "There Is Not a Friend like Jesus," and "To the End," which brought hope and inspiration to thousands of people. In 1979 Sheila recorded the uplifting song "Bright Sunshine." This record was a phenomenal success, selling 100,000 copies the first month on the market. Between 1980 and 1984 Sheila recorded the inspirational songs: "Jesus Will Never Leave You," "Trouble in My Way," "Old Time Faith," and "Calvary." These recordings brought her much money and fame. By 1986 Sheila was rich and famous and one of the top performers in the gospel world.

Although Sheila Mitchell had achieved fortune and fame in the gospel world, she hadn't done as well in the world of romance. Her relationships with men had been characterized by one word, "frustration." It seemed like the men who had been attracted to her just hadn't been her type, and the men she had been attracted to either had been after her money or had been intimidated by her success. However, there had been one exception. Her romance with Gary Thomas had been a good one for five years, but when he became tired of competing against her singing career he said to her, "Sheila, all of your singing and traveling prevents you from having enough time to spend with me. I'm tired of being second to your singing career. You are beautiful, charming, and rich, but I can't take being second anymore. Our relationship is over."

Sheila was stunned and hurt by Gary's sudden departure from her life. How could he be so insensitive to her feelings? Sheila was heartbroken for months after her break up with Gary, but she eventually got over it.

It was the spring of 1986 when Sheila finally met the man of her dreams. She met him at her cousin's wedding in Nashville. His name was Jason Hill. He was a wealthy businessman, tall and handsome, and thirty-three years old, four years older than Sheila. From the beginning, Jason was strongly attracted to Sheila. He made her feel like a queen, showering her with nice compliments, affection, and attention. He was not after her money nor was he intimidated by her success. He also didn't try to come ahead of her singing career. He just accepted Sheila for who she was; he didn't try to change her. By the time fall arrived, Sheila had been swept off of her feet by Jason's charm and affection, and was madly in love with him. However, she was not in love by herself; Jason was also madly in love with her. Whenever Sheila was out of town performing at gospel concerts, Jason would always call the hotel where she was staying and talk to her, telling her how much he loved her and how much he missed her.

Sheila and Jason continued their romance. As the months passed, their love for each other grew stronger and stronger. In June of 1988 they happily announced that they were going to get married. They set their wedding date for May 13, 1989.

When Sheila told her mother that she and Jason were engaged to get married, Mrs. Mitchell was all smiles. She said to Sheila, "Congratulations, baby, I believe you and Jason will make a nice couple."

Time moved fast as Sheila and Jason continued to enjoy their courtship. Soon it was May of 1989, the month of the wedding. One evening in early May, Sheila and Jason were eating supper at a restaurant when their conversation suddenly changed to their upcoming wedding. Jason said to Sheila, "Honey, our wedding date is approaching fast; within two weeks we will be husband and wife."

Sheila replied, "Jason, I can hardly wait for it to happen. I will be so happy when we become husband and wife. Our wedding date, Saturday, May 13 at 1:00 p.m., can't come fast enough."

On Friday May 12, Sheila went to bed early after a long, hard day of preparation for her wedding. Tomorrow was her wedding day and she wanted to be well rested for it. Around 1:00 a.m. Shelia was awaken by the ringing of the telephone. She picked up the telephone and said, "Hello, who is it?"

The caller replied, "Sheila, this is Denise, and I have some bad news to tell you about my brother, Jason. He was shot and killed last night around 11:00 p.m. as he was closing his service station. It was an apparent robbery attempt."

The tragic news about Jason's murder devastated Sheila, and she began crying hysterically. It took Mrs. Mitchell hours to console her.

After Jason's funeral, Sheila still continued to grieve over his murder. It was so difficult for her to give him up because she had loved him so much. She had been able to get over her father's accidental drowning back in 1969, although it hadn't been easy, but it seemed like she just couldn't get over Jason's death. She grieved day after day. One morning at breakfast she told her mother that she wasn't going to sing anymore because she wasn't in the mood for it. When Sheila's many admirers learned of her grief-stricken condition and of her decision to quit singing, they were shocked and saddened. In response, they sent her thousands of cards and letters offering her sympathy and encouragement. They also pleaded with her not to give up singing, but she was in such a grief-stricken state that they couldn't persuade her to change her mind.

Sheila continued to grieve over losing Jason, and eventually she withdrew into a shell. It deeply saddened Mrs. Mitchell to see her daughter in a shell. She tried to help her come out of it by encouraging her to give Jason up, but it didn't work. Sheila still continued to grieve over Jason. Mrs. Mitchell then turned to doctors for help. She spent lots of money going from doctor to doctor but none of them could help Sheila. She continued to grieve over Jason and to be withdrawn from the world.

Disappointed with the doctors, Mrs. Mitchell turned to prayer. She prayed day and night, asking the Lord to have mercy on her daughter and to enable her to get over Jason's death. Although Mrs.

Mitchell prayed day after day and night after night, Sheila continued to be depressed. She wouldn't go anywhere; she just stayed at home and grieved over Jason. When some people learned that Mrs. Mitchell was using prayer as a way to help Sheila, they were skeptical. They said, "If the doctors couldn't help Sheila Mitchell, prayer won't help her either." However, Mrs. Mitchell was not discouraged by the negative comments. She was a firm believer in prayer and she believed that it could change things. She, therefore, kept on praying, asking the Lord to bring Sheila out of her depression, and she kept on believing that He would.

One day Mrs. Mitchell asked Sheila to go shopping with her and to her surprise she said, "Yes, mama, I will go shopping with you."

Mrs. Mitchell's aim was to get Sheila out of the house so she could began to get Jason off of her mind. Sheila continued to go places with her mother, and after a while, Mrs. Mitchell could tell that she was slowly getting Jason off of her mind and was coming out of her shell. Next, Mrs. Mitchell was able to get Sheila to pray with her. The praying seemed to help Sheila and her condition improved more and more as the days passed.

It was a hot Saturday morning in June of 1992. Mrs. Mitchell was preparing breakfast when Sheila came into the kitchen and began singing the song "I Know What Prayer Can Do." Mrs. Mitchell was so happy to hear Sheila singing again that she joined in with her and they both sang "I Know What Prayer Can Do."

After they finished singing, Sheila said to Mrs. Mitchell, "Mama, I've given Jason up. I will no longer grieve over him. I'm going to go on with my life."

Sheila's words brought tears of joy to Mrs. Mitchell's eyes. She then said to Sheila, "Baby, you are a living witness to the power of prayer. I asked God to bring you out of that shell and He did. I am so happy that I feel like praising God. Thank you Jesus! Thank you Jesus!"

In August of 1992, Sheila Mitchell resumed her singing career after a three year absence from singing. Her many fans and admirers all over the gospel world were so happy to see her back singing again. At gospel concerts she would tell the audience how the murder of her fiance had caused her to be stricken with grief for three long years, and how she had been so despondent that she had felt like giving up, but through the power of prayer she had been able to overcome her grief and pain and resume her gospel singing career. These touching testimonies brought hope and inspiration to many people. Also at gospel concerts, Sheila would sang her heart out, and her beautiful singing voice would lift people's spirits and stir their souls. And wherever she sang the song "I Know What Prayer Can Do", New York City, Chicago, Los Angeles, or Miami, people cried, they shouted, and they ran up and down the aisles.

Being able to inspire and touch people through her singing was very rewarding to Sheila. There were a number of times when people walked up to her and told her that her singing had inspired them to turn their lives around. One time she was in the lobby of a hotel in Birmingham, Alabama when a woman with her eight children walked up to her and asked, "Are you the famous gospel singer Sheila Mitchell?"

Sheila answered, "Yes, I am."

The woman then said, "Sheila, my name is Margaret Finley and I am so glad to meet you. I didn't believe that I would ever get the chance to meet you so I could thank you for what you did for me. Your singing inspired me to turn my life around. I was on welfare with my eight children, living in a crime-infested housing project, when I heard you sing the song 'Jesus Will Fix It' on the radio, which made me believe that I could change my condition. And I did change my condition. I went back to school, got off welfare, and now I am a successful businesswoman. I own my own beauty salon."

Sheila commented, "Sister Finley, I am happy that I was able to help you. God has given me a talent for singing, and it is so wonderful that my singing inspired you to turn your life around. You take care of yourself and may God continue to bless you and your family."

Before Sister Finley and her children left the hotel, Sheila gave each one of them a big hug and told them good-bye.

Sheila continued to fill people's hearts with joy and inspiration wherever she sang and sometimes people would come up to her and tell her how much they thanked her for inspiring them to change their lives. One Sunday Sheila had sung at a church in Blytheville, Arkansas and was on the church parking lot with her entourage getting ready to drive to Little Rock when a man and his family came up to her. The man said, "Sister Mitchell, my name is Otis Henderson and I'm so happy to meet you. Will you please wait a few minutes so I can thank you for inspiring me to turn my life around?"

Sheila smiled and replied, "Sure, Brother Henderson, I have time to listen to you. Tell me your story."

Brother Henderson said, "You are not aware of it, Sister Mitchell, but your singing and testifying helped to change my life and I thank you so much. I was strung out on cocaine and was in bad shape. I was in and out of drug rehabilitation centers but none of them could help me overcome my drug addiction. I would be in the bed late at night and I would start craving cocaine. I tried to resist the urge to use cocaine but I didn't have the will power to resist it. I would then get out of bed and go snort some cocaine. My expensive cocaine addiction was very costly. I lost the nice home I was buying. I couldn't pay my car note and my beautiful Cadillac was repossessed by the auto dealer. My drug addiction also caused me to lose my job. I failed the drug test at my job and was let go. Most of my friends and relatives deserted me because they didn't want to be associated with a drug addict. Yes, I was in bad shape and didn't know what to do. I was seriously thinking about taking my own life and ending it all. But one Sunday, my wife asked me to come and go with her to a gospel concert here in Blytheville. I told her okay; I will go with you. I sat there in the church and listened to the different groups sing. Then, Sister Mitchell, you came up front to sing. But before you began singing, you told the church about how good God had been to you. You talked about how you had been in a state of depression for three long years and how God had brought you out of that state of depression. After you finished your testimony, you sang the song 'I Know What Prayer Can Do.' Your testimony and singing touched me, brought tears to my eyes, and lifted the heavy burden I was carrying. I said to myself if God enabled you to overcome your state of depression, then I believe God will enable me to overcome my drug addiction. From then on, each time I started to crave cocaine, I began praying to God, asking Him to give me the strength to resist that powerful urge to snort it. My prayers to God gave me the strength to resist that cocaine, and I overcame my drug addiction. I am now drug free. I am a living witness to the power of prayer and the goodness of God."

Sheila said, "Brother Henderson, you had a rough time with that cocaine addiction, but God brought you through it. I am so happy for you. Is this your wife and kids standing by your side?"

Brother Henderson replied, "Yes, Sister Mitchell, my wife and kids are right here by my side."

Sheila said, "You have a beautiful family, Brother Henderson."

Brother Henderson replied, "Thank you, Sister Mitchell, for your nice comments about my family. My wife and kids were very supportive of me when I had my drug problem. They never deserted me. I have some caring kids and a good woman."

Sheila laughed and asked, "Brother Henderson, I know you are treating your good woman right, aren't you?"

Brother Henderson smiled and answered, "Yes, of course, I am treating my baby right. I love and respect her so much. I will do anything for my wife."

Sheila said, "Well, Brother Henderson, my entourage and I have to leave for Little Rock now. It was so beautiful meeting you and your family. May God continue to bless you and your family. I will be here in Blytheville next spring. I hope you and your family come out to hear me sing."

Brother Henderson replied, "We will be there to hear you sing, Sister Mitchell. We wouldn't miss it for anything. Good-bye."

Sheila hugged Brother Henderson, his wife, and his kids before she got in her bus with her entourage. They then hit the highway heading to Little Rock for a gospel concert.

After singing in Little Rock, Sheila and her entourage headed west to Texas, where they sang in Dallas, Houston, Waco, Longview, Tyler, and other cities in Texas before heading back home to Nashville, Tennessee.

In August of 1994 Sheila was attending a revival at her cousin's church, where she was introduced to a handsome and well-dressed preacher named Marcus Boyd. He was a dynamic preacher who had long admired Sheila. In their conversation, Rev. Boyd told Sheila how much he liked and admired her. Sheila told him that she wasn't interested in romance but they could be friends. Rev. Boyd told her that he would be happy to be her friend. For weeks they had friendly conversations on the telephone, then one night during a conversation he asked Sheila could he take her to a movie. Sheila told him that because of her last tragic experience with romance, she wasn't interested in going to the movies, and she didn't know if she could ever love again. Rev. Boyd was dejected by Sheila's response but he told her he understood her situation.

About two weeks later, Rev. Boyd called Sheila again and asked her if he could he take her out to dinner. Sheila told him that she wasn't interested. But Rev. Boyd wasn't the type of man who gave up easily and he continued to ask Sheila to go out with him. But she would say no.

One night while talking to her best friend Melba, Sheila told her about Rev. Boyd and how he continued to ask her out for dinner, even though she always said no. Melba told Sheila that Rev. Boyd must really like her to keep on asking her out to dinner when he was repeatedly being rejected. Melba then said, "Sheila, I know you have had some negative experiences with love, but you can't give up. I believe that there still is a good man out there waiting for you. Rev. Boyd might be that man. But you will never know if you don't give him a chance. Go out with him."

Sheila replied, "Okay, Melba, I'll go out with him."

The night after her conversation with Melba, Sheila was called again by Rev. Boyd. As usual, he asked her could he take her out to dinner. To his surprise, Sheila told him yes. Sheila enjoyed her dinner with Rev. Boyd. She found him to be charming, full of fun, and a hearty eater. The two continued to date and they learned that they had a lot in common. When Sheila was out of town singing at concerts, Rev. Boyd would send her flowers and candy to show his affection for her. The two continued to grow closer, and by the summer of 1995, they were deeply in love with each other. In November of 1995, Sheila and Rev. Marcus Boyd announced that they were going to get married. They scheduled their wedding for May of 1996.

After scheduling their wedding date, Sheila and Rev. Boyd began making preparations for their upcoming wedding. They sent out invitations to friends and relatives. They also planned their wedding ceremony. Sheila chose her best friend Melba as her maid of honor. Rev. Boyd chose his best friend as his best man. Sheila's church, St. Mark Baptist, was chosen as the place of the wedding.

In May of 1996 in Nashville, Tennessee, gospel singer Sheila Mitchell and Minister Marcus Boyd were married before the largest crowd ever assembled at St. Mark Missionary Baptist Church. It was a very joyous occasion. Sheila was so happy that she had finally gotten married after years of frustration with romance. Rev. Boyd was happy because he had finally married gospel singer Sheila Mitchell, the beautiful and charming woman he had admired for over a decade. Mrs. Mitchell was the happiest person at the wedding. Sheila, her only child, had finally gotten married after all she had been through.

One cool day in early November of 1997, about a year and a half after the wedding, Sheila and Rev. Boyd were visiting Mrs. Mitchell's home when they told her they had a surprise for her. Mrs. Mitchell said to them, "Come on you all, don't keep me waiting, tell me what the surprise is."

Sheila replied, "Guess what, Mama! Marcus and I are looking forward to the birth of our first child in April of next year."

Mrs. Mitchell said in a very excited voice, "Hush your mouth, girl! You are telling me that you are pregnant. Oh, I am so excited! I can't wait until next year in April to see my first grandchild."

Time moved quickly and soon it was April of 1998, the month Sheila was supposed to have the baby. It was near the end of the month when Rev. Boyd took Sheila to the hospital to have the baby. On April 27, 1998 Sheila gave birth to twin boys. She named them Carl and Curtis.

When Sheila and the twins came home from the hospital, the first place Rev. Boyd took them was Mrs. Mitchell's house. The sight of the twin boys brought tears of joy to Mrs. Mitchell's eyes. She then looked at Sheila and Rev. Boyd and said, "I've been praying for this day to come for a long time. I am so happy that I feel like praising God. Thank you Jesus! Thank you Jesus!"

ANALYSIS OF STORY

This story "The Power of Prayer" is an illustration of the strength prayer can give a person if he believes. Gospel singer Sheila Mitchell was so depressed after the murder of her beloved fiancé, Jason Hill, that she went into a shell. Her mother, Mrs. Mitchell, took her to many doctors but they were unable to help her. Mrs. Mitchell then turned to prayer as a way of bringing her daughter back to her old self. Mrs. Mitchell prayed to God asking Him to give her daughter the strength "to give up Jason" so she could once again enjoy life. She also encouraged her grief-stricken daughter to pray with her. Eventually, prayer provided Sheila the strength "to give up Jason" and she went on with her life.

CONCLUSION

These five "spiritual stories" have dealt with people overcoming hard times and adversity through the power of hope and faith. In Story One "If You Believe It, You Can See It" it seemed like trouble was all in the way of Mrs. Mary Williams, her husband died, she had to struggle to support twelve children, and three of her sons got in trouble with the law. But being a strong, spiritual woman, she faced adversity with hope and faith, and overcame it. In Story Two "The Story of Job" Satan believed that Job was faithful to God only because things were going well but if things went bad, he would curse God to His face. God allowed Satan to test Job's faith with adversity. However, because of his strong faith in God, Job withstood the hardships brought upon him by Satan's evil tests. He also never renounced God; eventually God restored him to prosperity and happiness. In Story Three "The Lord Will Make a Way" Andre Walker faced numerous problems, including the loss of his job, his girlfriend, and his self-confidence, but through the power of faith he was able to turn his life around. In Story Four "Look on the Bright Side" basketball player Larry McNeil was able to sustain hope when things looked dark and gloomy by looking on the bright side of things. He was cut from his high school varsity basketball team and he encountered academic problems, which kept him from playing basketball. However, because he didn't give up he saw the bright side of basketball. He became a star high school basketball player and led his team to the state championship. In Story Five "The Power of Prayer" gospel singer Sheila Mitchell was stricken with grief by the murder of her beloved fiance, Jason, and slowly withdrew into a shell. Although the doctors couldn't help Sheila, her mother, Mrs. Mitchell, maintained hope through prayer. And she continued to believe that God was going to enable her daughter to overcome her condition. Eventually, through the power of prayer, Sheila gained the strength to give up Jason and get on with her life.

It is my hope that these "spiritual stories" can serve as a source of strength and inspiration to readers experiencing adverse conditions such as sickness, depression, frustration, imprisonment, drug addiction, and hopelessness. These stories don't have to impact a large number of people. If just one person is inspired to turn his or her life around from reading my stories, then all the time and energy spent creating them is well worth it.

Many times in life, gifted and talented people fail to reach their potential because when they encounter adversity they give up or fall apart. They lack the will to struggle through adversity. There have been athletes with the talent to make the pros but they gave up because of academic problems or other reasons. There have been students with the brains to get master degrees and Ph.D. degrees but they gave up when they encountered tough, demanding professors or other problems. Faith can give you the strength and will to face adversity and struggle through it. Hope can enable you to keep on struggling and believing when you feel like giving up.

Finally, these "spiritual stories" have been about the black experience. It has already been stated that the black experience "is a story of black people's struggle to overcome hard times and adversity in America from slavery to the present." The black experience is a story of a people enduring much pain and suffering over centuries, yet surviving. The black experience is a story of a people clinging to hope and faith when everything else was taken away from them. The black experience is a story of a people drawing strength and inspiration from prayers and songs. The black experience is a story of a people bouncing back again and again from setbacks and failures. The black experience is a story of a people overcoming overwhelming odds. Yes, the black experience is an inspirational story. It is a story waiting to be told.

ROBERT L. BRADLEY was born in Memphis, Tennessee. He is employed as a cartographer (mapmaker). He has been studying the history of black people since the fourth grade. He also enjoys writing short stories and poetry. He holds a B.A. degree in history from Tennessee State University of Nashville, Tennessee and a M.S. degree in geography from the University of Memphis (formerly Memphis State University).

STORIES ABOUT THE

BLACK
EXPERIENCE

THE LORD WILL MAKE A WAY

VOLUME ONE

To order a copy of this book, write to:

Robert L. Bradley
P.O. Box 25768
St. Louis, MO 63136